I0527310

Maria J. Bishop

Sunset Clouds

Maria J. Bishop

Sunset Clouds

ISBN/EAN: 9783337341879

Printed in Europe, USA, Canada, Australia, Japan

Cover: Foto ©Andreas Hilbeck / pixelio.de

More available books at **www.hansebooks.com**

SUNSET CLOUDS.

BY

MARIA J. BISHOP,

AUTHOR OF "THOUGHTS IN A SICK CHAMBER," "WORDS TO THE MARINER," "LETTERS TO A GOD-SON," "THE WOODLAND WALK," "HOURS WITH THE LONELY."

BOSTON:

PUBLISHED BY B. B. RUSSELL,

55 CORNHILL.

To Mrs. J. M. C.

DEAR MADAM:—

Will you permit me to associate your honored name with this trifling effort? feeling that whatever may be its reception by others, or its own deficiency, in your regard, it will meet with the kind conctruction with which you have ever distinguished its author.

Please accept it as a slight token of the sincere regard and deep respect with which I have the honor to be, Madam,

Yours gratefully,

M. J. B.

CONTENTS.

5

SUNSET CLOUDS.

THE NATIVITY.

'Tis midnight, and Judea's hills in placid beauty lay
As folds its wings o'er Palestine, the soften'd, silver ray.
And sweet Siloa's murmur, like a harp of liquid tone,
Rings on the heart its melody, in music faint alone,
And rushing Cedron, o'er its bed, seeks Jordan's peaceful
    wave,
And onward sweeps by Olivet, by king's and prophet's
    grave.
Judea's hills are glistening 'neath the pearly dews of
    night,
And on the whispering breezes, the palm-plumes quiver
    light;
O'er pastures, which the Psalmist praised, where stillest
    waters flow
The snowy flock reposes, and the shepherd wanders slow,

7

While through the arched heavens, one bright transcen-
    dent gem,
Floats on, on light's own pinion, to the walls of Bethle-
    hem.
A kingly train is moving across the desert far,
And brows where gleam the diadem are raised towards
    that star:
All, all is stillest silence, save the golden bridle's ring,
As o'er three princely forms unfold the banners of a king;
They come from distant Ararat, for prophecy has told,
A mighty one has risen, which nations shall behold.
Now bearing regal tribute, o'er distant deserts far
They hail with adoration, blest Jacob's silver star:
And now, an orb of living light, it burns in splendor,
    where
The mangers of a stable rude, a helpless infant, bear;
And now before that fragile form, bend low in homage
    there,
The wise, the mighty ones of earth, and pour the suppli-
    ant prayer.
Through hidings of deep poverty, the eastern pilgrims see
The Godhead bursting through its folds in bright Divin-
    ity,
As Judah's king their tribute gold, they lavish at his feet,
As Judah's God, their costly myrrh from India's thickets
    sweet,
For Israel's King is God *alone*, the Lord of earth and
    heaven,
And to his holy name, the sacred frankincense is given —
O Great Redeemer! we with them, in adoration lay

Before thy throne, the purest gold that love and faith can
    pay,
With myrrh of fervent praises, we thy holy name embalm,
While prayer, as sacred incense, shall thine earthly altars
    warm;
And while we seek thy dwelling, we feel that love's bright
    star
Which guides us through life's pilgrimage, is stationary
    there;
While Angel-harps are ringing the house of thine abode
Good will and peace "to sinful man," "All glory be to
    God."

THE SEA-SHELL.

Come trace awhile the sounding shore,
Where foot hath seldom trod,
And through the flashing surf explore,
The footsteps of a God.
Here, whirlwinds swell their sullen breath,
And lightning lances play.
While tempest speak the mandate, "Death,"
Or silenced, sink away.
How calmly grand the evening sky,
Where sunset's banner fell,
Yet all its purple pageantry,
Is burnished on this shell.

Some watch the tide of living gold,
Wafting the glory higher,

While to their minds the clouds unrolled
Are sentences of fire.
To them the stars are eloquent,
That thread the milky way,
And forest, lake, and mountain rend,
Like Memnon's statue play.
But softer tones across the sea
And liquid murmurs swell,
Dying away in melody
Within this sea-washed shell.

It tells us of that mighty Hand
That hollowed out the deep,
Chaining with links of silver sand
The billows headlong leap.
The citron grove and orange bower
Exhausted not his skill;
Not cedar bough or queenly flower,
Their Makers praise fulfill.
He bade the roaring, surging sea,
Sound soft as Sabbath bell,
Dying away in melody,
Within this sea-washed shell.

Seraphs may gaze in wondering love
Upon the dome of heaven,
While to the beaming eyes above
Are untold beauties given;
And to our eyes how fair ascends
Mount Blanca's brow of snow,
While morn, in golden veil attends
The Alpine pageants glow;

Touches of matchless beauty hide
In many a sylvan dell,
Less fair than white waves that glide
Around this silver shell.

THE MINISTRY OF THE SUFFERING.

THERE are various powers — mighty tal-. ents, loaned to mortals to work for Heaven, withall, in this poor world of ours. Each moving in its own orbit of usefulness or beauty, accomplishing its own peculiar ministry.

Yet perchance among the many mansions of moral grandeur reared for the human heart, there is not one which rears prouder towers than that filled by patient, submissive suffering.

The mind has its triumphs and wide is the sphere of its influence. Learning, power, beauty — all have their appointed work, yet they are not armed with the might — they wear not the diadem of glory which God hath bound about the brow of suffering.

We speak of misery with pity; we would alleviate trial and symphathize with affliction; yet, has Heaven laid all good on one side, all evil on the other? Not so. The sufferer treads a higher range than we, breathes a purer atmosphere and is conversant with the loftiest style of human thought.

True, the tearful eye, pale cheek and bowed form may seem to speak alone of weakness, decay and death, but look longer into the depths of those calm eyes — read you not there syllables higher than earthly language? gleams there not lights of strong truth, deep conviction and unearthly energy from the depths of that troubled spirit? More than this, far back of the trial, half-conscious to the sufferer, glow the rich beams of a peace the world knows not of, like the sunset hiding behind the storm.

How often, in the presence of some meek sufferer we feel a subduing awe, an atmosphere of moral grandeur. The world is delusive — all is real here; the world is vain and foolish; here is a wisdom breathed by

Omnipotence: "The golden sceptre of Heaven has touched this heart before us, and all bow down in this inner court of human sympathy."

THE ATTACK.

ON the confines of Dalmatia, lived, at the time our story commences, in an old, time-blackened cottage, the widow of a soldier, whose sole wealth consisted of her fair-haired child, the beautiful Hertha Wallenstein.

Arnold Wallenstein had been a brave man, and served his country well in the wars which the ambitious Frederick was ever waging; and when, at fifty, death found him on the battle-field, his piety, and a small, very small pension, became the heritage of the gentle pair, who still lived on in the half ruinous cottage, whose mouldering rafters drooped to the little garden, from which Hertha contrived to procure rose-leaves enough to exchange for that luxury, a little tea, wherewith to cheer the desponding hours of her mother.

On the evening when our story opens, the early twilight and drifting snowflakes had compelled Hertha to lay aside her needle earlier than usual.

The small table was neatly set forth before a cheerful fire, which glanced on the white forehead of Hertha as she moved with graceful activity about the apartment, while the eye of the widow was occasionally lifted from the Bible which rested on her lap, following, with a glance of love, the light, flitting form.

"I have a strange, dreary feeling to-night, mother dear," she said, "a sadness, almost terror, seems to beset me."

"Thou art lonely, my love," said the widow. "These sombre woods, and wild wastes of snow are little calculated to cheer a heart young as thine."

"Hark, mother, was not that a distant horn?" as she flung the hair from her temple, and paused to listen.

"Thou art listening, dear, for Walter. He

will not be here to-night, for see, how the storm gathers. The very kittywakes are flying to shelter, and that betokens rough weather."

At the name of her lover, Hertha's cheek deepened its color, and she turned again to her household duties. In a moment she started.

"Surely, mother, there are strange sounds in the distance. Thine ear is dull, but mine heard something then like a human cry of pain."

They were interrupted by the entrance of a young man. His face was flushed and his whole manner was excited, while his fine features worked with emotion.

"I come," he said, "to place you in safety," turning to the widow, "Hertha, you must fly, I scarce know whither. The Cossacks have attacked the village, at the foot of the pass, and their ruthless cruelty spares neither sex nor age. We have not one moment to lose. They will be here in half an hour.

As he spoke, he was busy undoing from its place on the wall, where it had been suspended since the death of its owner, the short carbine which had once made terrible havoc in these same Cossack ranks.

The widow, whose cheek had blanched at his tidings, arose calmly, and laid her hand upon his arm.

"Walter," she said, the sweet voice scarcely broke, "leave that weapon. Our trust must not be in earth-steel. A higher arm than thine must defend us. Stop, my son!" for still the young man pulled at the thongs that bound it.

"Mother," he said, "this is madness. I outsped the chamois to secure your safety, leaving bow and buckler behind. The age of miracles is past! I must have this to defend Hertha, if I must not use it for you."

"Walter," she replied, "I do not quit this cottage; neither shall Hertha. Heaven can protect us here. To fly is but to meet those brutes the sooner."

"Mother, you are wild! Fly, fly to the

forest, while life may yet be saved," he said. A wild, piercing shriek of agony, mingled with yells, which sounded like those of wild beasts, came distinctly born on the breeze.

Hertha sank, almost fainting, by the side of the widow, whose bloodless cheeks confessed her fears.

"Not yet, unto martyrdom," she said, as she took the sacred volume.

"You hear!"

The words were groaned out between the closed teeth of Walter, as the terrible cries came appallingly near.

"It is now too late!" and he threw himself on a settle, burying his face in his hands. "My Hertha, my Hertha! how can I yield thy life to yonder wolves?" he groaned.

Louder and louder rose the cries, while mother and daughter, their arms wound around each other, sat pale as marble statues.

All was silent in the cottage save the occasional murmured prayer of the widow, while the ticking clock marked the minutes, that seemed hours.

" Those cries are becoming distant," and Walter raised his head from the attitude of despair into which he had fallen. " Can it be possible that, slaked with blood, they have left the village ? "

" Said I not that Heaven would defend us ? " replied the matron.

Through the long night they sat, and when, at length, the hour told of daylight, still all was darkness.

Impatient of captivity, Walter opened cautiously the barred door. A wall of snow fenced the humble entrance, which had effectually blotted out the existence of the cottage to those without.

" You were right, mother," he said, " a better defence than the rusty carbine has shielded your head."

It was some hours before he could make his way through the marble drift, and when, at length, he struggled down the path, he was soon met by a detachment of Prussian soldiers, whose uniform of green was fair to him as the wings of angels.

Arrived at the village, whose beauty had long lured the summer traveller, blackened walls, and blood-stained ruins told its terrible fate. The stiffened forms of its late inhabitants lay here and there; the girl clinging in death to the white haired sire. Not a single house was spared. Even over the frozen brook the trampled snow was mingled with a crimson stain, while the few modest ornaments that decked the dwelling of the pastor, were strewn in mockery among the smoking ruins.

It was long ere Widow Wallenstein could leave her dwelling, now guarded by the imperial troops; and when, at last, she passed in her way to greater security, the home of her youth, she raised her eyes, devoutly saying,

"The Lord is a defence."

THE DEATH OF THE FIRST-BORN.

Around the towers of Thebes the night has drooped her
    sable wing,
Canopied with darkness, fold the pillow of a king.
That day, in anger fierce, he bade the prophets of the
    Lord,
No more, in Heliopolis, to list a monarch's word.
Death is their doom — if they shall dare again to seek
    his face;
Death is the doom! the angels now have sealed the day
    of grace.
'Tis midnight—and on rapid wing the angel herald flies—
In lowly tent and palace hall the best beloved dies.
In peaceful Goshen's balmy vales he sheathes his flaming
    sword,
For door and lintel, crimsoned there, are guarded by his
    God.
The angel stoops to listen to the Hallel's holy strain,
That prays he may pass over, where the chosen lamb is
    slain.
He spreads his mighty pinions — each mother clasps her
    son.
As passing over Israel, he wings to splendid On.
Here, bloodless, stands the portal-arch; the angel enters
    there —

A queenly mother starts from sleep, and tears her raven
    hair;
From Pharaoh's brow, the haughty frown in sorrow wild
    has fled,
For Egypt's pride, his princely boy, his eldest-born, is
    dead!
Through Egypt's realm a cry ascends,— the beautiful are
    gone,
And infants fair from many a mother's bleeding heart are
    torn!
The warder at the palace gates, bows low his plumed
    head,
As by him swift, on mission wing, the herald angel sped.
The slaves to her bare bosom clasps her bright and beau-
    teous boy,
His fainting head she strives to stay,— he was her sunset
    joy;
And priestly forms in agony bend o'er the young and fair,
And wildly cry to Egypt's gods their best beloved to
    spare,
While blood-stained robe, and magic ring, and severed
    locks declare
How more than unavailing they deem their anguished
    prayer.
On, speeds the mighty vengeance! the murmured wail
    ascends
As o'er a slaughtered little one each dark-browed mother
    bends.
Even in the green pastures sinks down the snowy lamb,
And sobs in dying agony beside its meek-eyed dam.

The sun on rebel Egypt in morning splendor broke,
But many a long-lashed lid, its beams no more to gladness
    woke,
Bearing the loved ones of the heart move many a mourn-
    ing train
On to the Nile's still waters, across the burning plain;
And as the bright and flashing waves the youthful corpses
    bear —
The slaughtered infants of the Nile seem hovering in the
    air:
And Pharaoh, who to Cheop's pile his best beloved hath
    given,
Must in the wave its diadem soon render back to heaven.
From heaven rings — as *thou* hast done, it shall be done
    to thee —
As the last plumed helmet sinks beneath the gurgling sea.

ENDURANCE.

THE quality of meeting, with settled calmness and fortitude, the difficulties and trials of life, is, perhaps, as rare as it is valuable. Life is a checkered scene, and it has many sweet oases scattered along its path; there are likewise narrow defiles, sharp rocks, and steep precipices, to scale which, requires a steady eye and intrepid heart.

Those periods of existence which are unmarked by difficulty, are passed over quickly, or rather, glide by us with an imperceptible tread; while the emergency which is the real, as well as the severest test of character, is sure to come, presenting obstacles and inciting to efforts which only the heart nerved to endurance can meet with composure.

We speak of the great. Who are they? The benefactors of mankind, who have stood foremost in life's battle, are undoubtedly entitled to the name; yet there are a host of nameless heroes, who, perchance, in the eye of Heaven, are crowned with chaplets greener than they; those who have met difficulties, fears, discouragements, and day after day grappled with, silently endured and overcame them.

There is something morally sublime in the spectacle of a brave heart, encompassed by a sea of trials, yet relying upon Heaven and its own nobleness, bearing calmly; and it presents a clue to what we call the dark dealings of Providence, that its sternest discipline is often reserved for those whose patience is most proof. Many a character which would have remained unknown, has by this means been presented as a shining light before the eyes of others, or rather, has been formed — cut as the diamond stone, from the quarries of its darkened nature, by sharp touches of adversity.

This valuable trait of character, far from being formed, as many suppose, by the pressure of great calamities, is nourished and supported by the recurrence of those daily and petty trials which are more or less the lot of all. The meek bearing of an injury, the support of some lonely trial, form the pedestal which upholds the " column of true majesty " in our nature.

Vain would it be to secure for the young the most affluent gifts of fortune, the rarest endowments of education, or hosts of friends, while they are strangers to this element of character; none can help us, as we can help ourselves, and the heart which ever leans on others for support and comfort, has but a miserable chance of happiness or usefulness. Teach the young the mighty lesson to bear, and thereby they are instructed to *do;* and when the day of trial comes, a firm hand is laid upon the helm, and a patient spirit looks up to Heaven for deliverance.

This virtue formed a mighty element of character in the lives of Franklin, Howard, and all who have laid a giant hand on the difficulties of life. Much of life may pass as a calm, summer day ; but the wise mariner puts out to sea with chart and compass, as well as with sail spread to the favoring breeze; and by constant sounding, searches for the hidden rock. And thus, while the sunshine of prosperity gilds the surface of character, it is the storm alone which tests its real strength, conducing most to the permanent good of man, and the glory of God.

THE USE OF TALENTS.

HAS the reader reflected, that the Lord gave to each servant, at least, one precious gift — one talent. Has it occurred to him that of all the many million servants, there is not one that has not some treasure wherewith he may traffic for Heaven?

The knowledge of the fact of having received a talent, adds greatly to the power of rightly improving it; the feeling of having received a trust, in every honorable mind awakes integrity, decision, effort; and this truth, received into the mind and retained there, that some gift is lodged in every bosom, some power in every soul, would nerve to exertions and animate to success, of which one might think themselves incapable.

The thought that an achievement is possible, produces the effect of which it is the cause; the conviction that we have the means within our reach of attaining an object, leads to ultimate success.

This conviction ploughed for Columbus a path across the deep, and landed him in the wished-for haven; this has brought forms of life-like beauty from the cold marble; has caused visions of transcendant loveliness to float across the canvas, and inanimate nature, moulded by the thought that a gift was bestowed, has leaped into creations of consummate perfection.

The belief that each is the recipient of some great and beautiful gift; some talent for which account must be rendered, would lead to much wisdom in the choice of professions for the young, and to much economy in the use of time. The mind readily grasps that for which it is fitted by nature; the knowledge of it is easily acquired, and its practice yields continual pleasure; whereas the faculties, in a direction to which they are forced, are dull and heavy, and life passes constant constraint and discontent.

Let every parent consider that his child has a talent for music, for painting, for architecture, or for domestic economy; and against their will, let the world lose a working hand, and gain a working mind, or spoil a fine lady in making a useful woman.

The knowledge that God has bestowed upon every human mind a peculiar adaptation to some particular subject; powers and faculties fitted in a high degree for some congenial object, will, of itself, carry the soul a flight above others in the pursuit of it.

That which is regarded as the "ten talents of genius," is often little more than one moderate talent improved by industry; winged by love of its labor, urged on little by little, it makes .its way, it gains on its course, and is continually rewarded by added gifts and opportunities of usefulness.

This one talent often lies by in indolence, and buried deep under a weight of earthly cares, which would disappear, were it but used.

Draw but the hidden treasure from its envelope. Ask yourself the question: "For what has Providence peculiarly fitted me?" And then give yourself to the work with your whole energy, and give not over the pursuit of some worthy object, by means of those powers which you, and perhaps none so well as you possess.

But this subject also includes opportunities as well as gifts of intellect or heart. God, who gives the mental talent, gives also opportunities for its development; and it is interesting, in this connection, to watch life and perceive how the shepherd, by gathering pebbles from the brook of Bethlelem, and hurling them successfully against the lion which attacks him, is thus taught by his

God to defend his people; and how Luther, the poor monk, whose efforts are humbly given to dust and to arrange a library, finds arguments on its shelves for a reformation.

Thus it will ever be that He, who bestows the gift, will make a way in which we may traffic with the same; happy they who appreciate the gift and seize the opportunity for its use; to such, shall, indeed be added, " the plume to the wing, the gem to the crown, the city to the sceptre!"

ANCHORED.

You say that it is not able,
  Faith, in the surges of life,
To hold, like a gallant cable,
  In the billows' angry strife.

You say, when the winds are sleeping,
  And the glassy wave is still,
The heart may trust to its keeping,
  But *not* in the days of ill;—

That when the surges dashing,
  Roll the angry waves around,

Faith parts its cable, crashing,
  The wreck is fast *aground.*

You say, but after the shipwreck,
  What help in the iron thews?
Still true to the broken hawser,
  Deep down 'mid the sea-weed and ooze.

There are who have known while the breaker
  Was washing the deck amain,
The hand of the mighty Maker
  Was grasping the broken chain.

Though plank from plank was riven,
  And the mast had crashed o'er the side,
The anchor was moored in heaven,
  And the wreck must stem the tide.

Is it better? one spar of memory
  To the billow-beaten crew,
Than the cheer of the heavenly life-boat,
  " Fear not, I will bear you through!"

The promise that rings to landward,
  Through all this darkness and pain;
The narrow ridge in the graveyard,
  Blooming, shall open again; —

And yours, to be parted never,
  With its beauty of deathless hair,
By your side to move forever,—
  An angel head bends there.

Death is the foam of the billow,
 Death is the roar of the tide;
Faith sweeps like a bending willow,
 Fast moored to the other side.

Think not thy cable parted,
 See it flash through the broken spray;
Each plank in the ship, though started,
 Shall ride in the golden bay.

And there, with a joyous greeting,
 Is the beautiful, deathless brow,
At rest, while the storm you where beating,—
 That sleeps in the distance now.

CULTIVATION OF THE INTELLECT.

BY the cultivation of the intellect, is not intended those artificial refinements of society, and elaborate accomplishments which are within the reach of but comparatively few, but rather those solid foundations of useful knowledge and that enlightened mind which are equally desirable, as they are within the reach of all.

But particularly is it desirable that the female heart, enlarged by charity, should be directed by an intelligent and active mind — a mind accustomed to enlarged and just modes of thinking ; capable of directing the young and the ignorant with whom her position throws her in contact.

Unconnected with a sound judgment, a sensibility so tremblingly alive that it renders itself and all around it uncomfortable — much more an effected love of the beautiful, are sure to tire and render home, which should be the centre of earthly interest, dull and unattractive ; and yet how few females are there, comparatively, whose minds are equal to draw a deduction or to carry on an argument on the high and sublime truths with which, as rational beings, they are connected.

There are those so unhappily mistaken as to suppose that a cultivated understanding is unnecessary for a woman, at least, that it diminishes in some degree that humility and modesty which are her ·chief charms. Is then, the Moslem right? and should all which is lofty and ennobling be confined to those who least need it? No! mind was given to woman, and with the responsibility and duty of cultivating it; to woman is committed in a good degree the moral government of the world, and therefore a high order of attainment should mark that being who has its moral moulding.

The next point for consideration is what studies — what pursuits are the easiest, the surest and the most general means towards the attainment of an end so desirable.

Without pausing to rest the argument upon the study of the sciences or a general acquaintance with belles-letters, which, unquestionably are as important for females, or nearly so, as for the other sex, we should hasten to enter a field with which the villager and the princes are alike surrounded; to pierce a mine, whose flashing glories gem, alike, the brow of the humble and the high.

The Volume of Inspiration spreads its transcendent page alike before the eyes of all, and we contend that the mind, set to grapple with its high and momentous truths, can never again be dwarfed to its former ignorance; take, for instance, the eternity of God, as the standard to which we would tower the intellect, and you extend it in the vain attempt to grasp the immensity of the thought.

There is, also, another fact, connected with the study of Scripture, which renders it the fitting library of the young, as well as the exhaustless treasure of the aged; it is the extreme beauty of its conceptions, united with the grandeur of its language; let this stand as an example: "He that inhabiteth the praise of Israel;" surely, any mind, alive, in the least, to the truly sublime and beautiful, cannot but muse in mute admiration at the figure, which makes the lofty chants of adoration the holy pavilion of the Deity; and we contend, that the thought which buds in the mind from such seed as this, must needs be inimitable and pure.

It may seem trite and common-place advice to send all to the Bible, for is not the Bible in the hands of all? yes, but how few study it! Perused carelessly, it perhaps does little but add condemnation to the reader; for it is irreverance to read it carelessly; but deeply studied, it is a map of light, unfolding labyrinths of length and glory far into the limitless fields of eternity. Such effects will — must follow the study of the Word of God; add to this an intelligent observation of the beauties of creation, and an awakened sensibility to all, the mind will take a wide range, and be tuned to a lofty key; sources of refined pleasure will be opened to those who have received the benefit of educational culture, and a world of satisfaction, pure and high, will open before the minds of all.

ALONE.

Alone by the sea-shore, alone by the lake,
Alone in the desert or African brake:
By Thebe's ruined arches, or Babylon's stone,
Where the slow floating eagle shrieks ever alone.

There are sylvan retreats that the Hermit has sought,
There are rocks where the chamois the hunter has taught,
But earth holds no desolate corner apart
So lonely, so sad as a desolate heart.

Alone in the crowd, as the Jordan's blue wave
Cuts the dark waters by it, but only to lave
His waters alone to the far, distant sea,
Mingling, yet separate — fettered, yet free.

We may meet on the mountain, may meet in the glen,
In the kindness, compassion and kindred of men:
But where, in the world's crowded mart, shall we find
Communion of feeling, and mingling of mind?

There's a world all aglow with all beautiful thoughts,
There feeling and memory and sympathy bright
Cluster and linger and glitter, and seem
Like the vistas of light in a glorious dream.

And there, though in solitude, joyous we live
In peace, that the Author of mercy can give,
And joys, to the spirit full often atone —
Who walks with his God can be never alone.

THE PRIZE.

The last canvass had separated the gentry of the neighborhood of Wildersly, and it was fast becoming a painful question by what means they should again be brought to a right feeling. At length the happy expedient of an archery meeting was hit upon, and a committee appointed to confer upon the happy theme. Great was the joy of the stately mammas and bright-eyed daughters of Wildersly; but as it was not to them, but to their grave papas, that the sage question was deferred, it progressed more slowly than the zealous wished.

Subtle points came up to be disputed at the club dinner. First, who should be invited; and as it was to be a thoroughly respectable affair, none but undoubted gentry were to be admitted. Then the question came up among the squires, "What is a gentleman?"

Some one defines it one who has plenty of money. Another, "He who has retired from business ten years."

But as the first would admit Mr. Shorts, whom no one could endure, and the second would exclude General Vendables, who had never been in business, but who was universally acknowledged as an undoubted gentleman, the committee were thrown on their own resources.

There were, moreover, sundry little hates; bitter as those of Highlanders, and handed down with the faithfulness of the Capulets, to be tenderly dealt with. Among these private feuds were those of the Vendables and Browns, which had increased in the same ratio that the fine old trees of the Vendables had changed owners, passing into the hands of the more fortunate Mr. Brown, whose display of mere wealth was a sharp thorn in the side of his aristocratic neighbor.

At the time our story opens the old feud had descended, as a sort of heirloom, to General Aubrey Vendables, who had just returned from foreign service on leave of absence.

Great was the joy of Lucy, the sister of our hero, as the archery meeting drew nigh; and loud was she in praises of her friend Emmeline Brown, as she strolled with her brother beneath the fine old oaks of the manse.

"I cannot think," exclaimed Aubrey, on one of these occasions, "how it is these Browns have so risen in favor? Pray, does Miss Emmeline inherit her father's want of beauty, or her mother's vulgarity?"

"You deserve not to be answered," replied Lucy, a tear trembling in her eye. "Emmeline is just a rosebud."

"Of the cabbage species, I presume," replied the general.

Lucy drew her arm from his, and for once was really provoked with her handsome brother.

"Seriously, Lucy, tell me why it is that my mother and yourself are determined so spitefully to like these Browns. I thought we had all agreed to hate them."

"Yes, brother, but when papa died, there was that lawsuit. Mr. Brown dropped it at once."

"Might be policy," was the curt reply.

"Then the butler was dishonest, and Mr. Brown defended mamma's rights; and when the man was condemned, at our entreaty, mitigated his sentence."

"That showed him merciful," replied Aubrey.

"Really, Aubrey, you are too bad! Then mamma had the quinsy, and Mr. Brown mounted his fleetest horse, and went miles for the physician who saved her life."

"I am vanquished — I can say no more," said the general. "But, dear Lucy, do not press your sweet Emmeline upon my notice."

Lucy blushed and was silent.

* * * * *

The morning of the archery meeting dawned

beautifully, and at an early hour the grounds of Walton Hall were thronged with groups of the young people of the vicinity. Green and silver was the not unbecoming costume of the occasion ; and young girls in delicate fabrics, and their stately mothers in brocade and pearl jewelry, might be seen threading the avenues of the park.

As Vendables greeted the lord of the manor, who was an old friend of his father, he was somewhat disturbed by a slap on the shoulder, and turning, beheld his old enemy, Mr. Brown. Constraining himself, he returned the rude shake of the hand, with mere cold politeness bowing to Mrs. Brown, who, in rouge and good humor, looked like a full-blown peony. At a little distance, as if retreating from notice, stood a beautiful girl. The soft brown hair thrown back from a faultless forehead, the blue eyes veiled by their long lashes, and the sweet expression of the lips, betokened a heart kind and true. Her dress was of the palest shade of green silk, and silver acorns were woven as its finish. A garland of oak leaves was twisted in her hair, and at her side hung a small silver quiver. Aubery colored as Lucy presented him to her friend, and he soon returned to greet Mr. Brown more cordially.

Among the competitors for the prize it was soon found none were to be named with Lucy and her friend; and loud and long was the applause as the arrow of Emmeline struck that of Lucy within the ring. The prize was to be awarded after a slight collation, and as competitors, Lucy and Emmeline alone remained.

When all were again gathered on the green, Emmeline could not be found; and Lucy, declaring that she would not take advantage of this circumstance, wandered to the verge of the forest, where an artificial cascade flung its music on the air. Seated on the spreading root of an aged oak, she here found her friend, and the two, happy in each other's company, soon forgot their mock conflict.

" O Lucy, you dear good girl! How kind

of you to send my dress; and your felicitous taste is so charming. I have not yet expressed the obligation I am under."

"Not nearly as lovely as the roses you sent mother last spring, for which I leave Aubrey to thank you, as he is coming this way."

"The bearer of good tidings, fair ladies," he said, turning in his hand a beautiful richly-chased silver arrow, which he presented, with a bow, to Emmeline.

"O no," she said, "Lucy was the successful candidate. I retired from the field."

"Nevertheless, young lady, it has pleased the judges to award the *first* prize to you; but as Lucy was second only to yourself, she also has an arrow." And he plunged a similar weapon through the golden locks of his sister.

"Really, general, I cannot receive it," Emmeline replied. "It is not just."

"Let your father settle the point," he replied. "I also shall claim a prize!" and he drew her reluctant arm within his own. "Mr. Brown," he said, approaching the old gentleman, who, weary with the labors of the day, was sitting alone, " your daughter refuses the prize. Will you bestow it upon me, but with it the hand that holds it ? "

Mr. Brown looked from one to the other; then, with a smile lighting his benevolent face, placed the hand of Emmeline in that of Vendables.

THE RUINS OF POMPEII.

Proud city of the dead! thy shadowy glory
   Steals sadly from the past; a spectral thing:
Long had the sandal of the world pressed o'er thee,
   While calmly wrapped beneath oblivion's wing —
Lost to the rival legions o'er thy head,
Rearing high arches o'er thy sleeping dead!

Rising, at length, above the funeral pall,
   Speaking, in trumpet tones, "*Mortality!*"
Telling the nations they shall likewise fall
   In all the purple of their majesty,
And banners blazoned with imperial pride
Flash and then sink beneath oblivion's tide.

Here is the dint the gilded chariot made,
    As, thundering o'er thy ways, the victor came;
And there the burden of the slave is laid,
    Who *lived* unknown, and found in *death* a name;
And there the mother who, in agony,
Would clasp her children for eternity.

Here stands the column speaking Cæsar's pride,
    And there the dwelling of deep poverty;
The marble roof where Roman matron died,
    When dark and darker the Italian sky
Frowned, while Jehovah, in a fiery car,
Triumphed o'er Jove, and drove his demon crew afar.

Mighty in wisdom, did thy Pliny stand,
    Watching the heavings of that blackened sea,
Scorching and withering the vine-clad land,
    Bow his high head, and lay him down with thee,
And o'er *thy* grave, his monumental name
Erect, as funeral trophy to thy fame?

Amid thy columns grand, and broken arches,
    Flashes the splendor of a bygone age;
With sandalled tread the Roman legion marches,
    Where History unrolls her burning page,
The classic toga and the glittering helm,
    Ages of ruin cannot yet o'erwhelm.

The Dacian captive with his calm, pale face,
    His arm unbound to deal the deathly blow,
Or Christian gladiator, who can trace,

Neither in savage nor in Greek a foe,
Thy arena's blood-stained pavement meekly trod,
Firm in the faith and calmly died for God.

Dark mistress of the world! thy jewelled brow
Still flashes its tiara worn and dim,
And from its time-stained circlet, broken *now,*
In martyr's blood its jewels seem to swim;
And as we muse thy strange stone tablet's o'er,
Even pity bids thee sleep and wake no more.

ENERGY.

TO no purpose are the highest talents bestowed, if energy is wanted in the employment of them. Energy is to the human mind, the same as the conducting belt is to machinery; it links the active power with the useful purpose, making the man mighty for good.

If sloth and inactivity are suffered to clog the spirits and benumb the understanding, it is in vain that the rarest opportunities combine with brightest intellectual graces, no fruit will ever be harvested — nay, no harvest of thought will ever adorn the barren, useless life; a mere mechanical movement in the round of duty; doing, because compelled by necessity, is all which such a state of mind can produce.

But let energy enter the heart and hand, and the pulses beat with a nobler bound; life is beheld as a rare opportunity for doing good — acting for the future, a golden field of unreaped purposes waving in the light of eternity. Duties are performed with alacrity; difficulties are grappled with a master-spirit; even positive misfortunes are borne with an easy cheerfulness. The heart is at ease, moulding circumstances which would crush others; only enobled by those trials which are the appointed discipline and education of a mighty spirit. In meek dependence upon Providence the energetic spirit trusts; in firm reliance on its own efforts it executes, and raises from the barren rock of Adversity a little garden of thoughts and purposes and noble deeds, all smiling under its life-giving power.

Energy has cut to the heart of the earth, and bound its ribs in its own diadem. Energy has united the earth, long divided for want of it, while continents arose at its bidding : it has trodden, as it were, the arches of Heaven, gazed down on the rainbow, counting its dyes; chained the lightning to its car, and bade it go, its willing, speaking messenger ; but greater still — it has taught the tried heart to look up to the God who made it, and overcome the evils of this troublesome life.

EQUALITY.

THAT all are created free and equal is a maxim rather expressed than felt, and while all concur in admiring the sentiment, almost all render it practically useless.

Inherent nobility is the exploded error of the old world ; that the son should be great because his father was, has been too often contradicted by his being a fool. Some

" Village Hampden," great in conscious right, meets the imbecile prince, curbs his tyrannic power, and wrests forever from him the argument that the mighty are great in virtue of their pedigree.

While it is ordered in the dispensation of Providence that some should rule and some should obey, it is equally manifested by those dispensations that " righteousness exalteth a people," that " the diligent shall bear rule," but " the slothful shall be under tribute."

In spite of the benign influence of republican institutions, the diligent observer must perceive a growing degree of adultation paid to wealth and the trappings of success. " The poor man by his wisdom may deliver the city," yet it is counted genteel not to remember that same poor man. Merit in a chariot is heralded by public applause; but merit in a plain garb is hardly allowed foothold among the sternest difficulties of life.

Now, in contradistinction to this, Providence often parts the ranks of ostentatious nothingness, to make a way to the front for the meek, the wise, and the good. Like a kind father, distributing justly to his children, Heaven has given to each some special gift. True, the gift may be unknown to the possessor, "wrapt in a napkin," or worse, misused; but it is nevertheless a gift which, were it drawn forth and put to proper interest, would redound to the glory of the Giver, and the good of man.

Viewed in this light, society presents a different surface from that which modern taste and modern manners has assigned. We feel the man is to be valued for what he is, not for what he possesses; except as those possessions mark his industry, genius, or integrity.

Virtue is the "image and superscription of Heaven," and when we honor it we honor God; but fortune is but the Cæsar of this world, and we render it fitting homage when we treat it with indifference.

CHRISTMAS.

The Christmas chimes
Of olden times,
Through leafless branches sigh and quiver,
And frost-work bright,
And soft moonlight,
Adown the forest arches shiver.
The midnight sky
Is jewelled high,
Wearing a cornet of glory;
While orbs of fire
And angel's lyre,
Bring forth to-night the Bethlehem story.

The chancel wide
Is wreathed in pride,
And the dim aisles like pine groves whisper;
While silvery note
And anthems float
Through the high dome like angels' vesper.
And earth to-night
Is fair and white,
With fleecy bridal-veil adorning;
Brake, bush and bower,
Spire and tower,
Waiting the flashing joy of morning.

Ye bright orbs say
Which is the ray
That over Bethlehem burned in beauty:
That o'er the plain
Drew princely train,
To own their king in lowly duty?
And did the moon
At midnight's noon
Look then as now, so calm and holy?
While angel's wing
And welcoming,
Soft sank beside the manger lowly.

The same are they
As bright to-day
As when "to us a Son was given ! "
Be our refrain
The angel strain —
"Good will to man and peace from Heaven ; "
Light the glad hearth,
Through joyous earth,
While merry Christmas bells are ringing;
Spread high the feast
Though poor the guest,
For earth with angels now is singing

THE VALUE OF TIME.

OF all the possessions which man can call his own, none is so little estimated and so fleeting as time. As if to impress with more emphasis its great worth, one lonely moment is granted and no more, at once. However wisely persons may judge respecting the whole of life — whatever calculations they make for its improvement of the several parts of which life is made — all are inclined to be prodigal. Well has it been remarked by the philosopher: "That to many, time appears as a vast desert, with here and there an oasis scattered up and down, bearing no proportion to lonely wastes over which they must travel. Hence the inconsistency of wishing away days and weeks, that the desired situation may be gained. Vainly will any rightly estimate time, who are not careful of its hours and minutes. Those spare moments which are ever recurring in the midst of the most crowded occupations are often that upon which the moral of life turns. The habit of procrastination — of deferring to 'a more convenient, the duties and enterprises of life — is one of the most mischievous which can possess the mind. That period of settled leisure seldom or never arrives, and even if old age should offer such a calm, is its enfeebled powers, its gathering infirmities, proper antecedents for any great work? The heart that rightly values time, that daily considers for what purpose life is given, will devote it, as it passes, to the highest, noblest ends. Among its fitting employments are the acquisition of knowledge and the pursuit of virtue; aud by slow and almost imperceptible degrees, the traveller advances in both these paths. Each day some new truth added, some attainment made in excellence is the only way to make time the treasury which it is to every well-balanced mind.

To have an end — a life-purpose high and

holy, such as shall glorify God and benefit man, is an essential, almost a lonely element of happiness. To feel that the hours as they pass, are filled with worthy purposes, and hastening forward a desired end — is, of itself, a world of pure joy. Virtue is not only its own reward; but like a pure stream, it leaves beauty and prosperity in its path, and hours redeemed from the past, given to the excellent, have a powerful and fertilizing effect upon our future life. The restlessness of a heart forever seeking novelty, the desire of fame, and the thirst for fleeting pleasures, is checked in a mind which is ever at home in its duties, that sees life too, made of parts, and beholds in every opportunity, a fresh call to exertion. The hours never hang wearily upon their hands, who place upon this heavenly talent its fitting value. They prize them as the garner of future joy, the witnesses for or against them. To such, a day is a loan, to trade for heaven with; in it they can, perhaps, bind up some bleeding heart, right some injustice, or further some worthy cause, and while the vain and idle complain of slow progress, they seize, improve, and multiply their hours. But in no season of life does this truth speak with a voice so eloquent as in youth. In youth the calls to duty are strongest, the encouragements to effort brightest; and if youth is thus used as time that must be accounted for, the honors and influence of more advanced life will be the natural results. Every season of life filled by its appointed duty, will leave the mind that true calm and leisure of soul in which alone is found real peace.

IN MEMORIAM.

All thy leaves of fading fern,
Sleeping Poet deck thy urn!
All thy brilliant, burning thought,
To thy sepulchre are brought.

Did thy Lord, in mercy free
With ten talents dower thee
Like a beacon's light to burn —
Gentle, brilliant Fanny Fern!

Thine the glance — the Prophet's eye
Moral, mental worth to spy;
Thine the tongue, with Prophet's fire,
Tuning words like well-strung lyre.

Who, with radiant thoughts, like thee,
With thy own wild witchery
Could make beautiful and true
Sparkle like the Summer dew?

Through the land soft requiems sigh
When its gifted daughters die;
When such minds as Parton's fail,
Who shall wear the prophet-veil?

Drinking at the fountain deep,
With thy sister-poets sleep,
While the fern leaves grow o'er thee,
Carey and sweet Signourney.

God, that sweeps the human soul,
And the burning thoughts control,
While He fills His shining choir,
Still shall waken some sweet lyre.

RETIREMENT FAVORABLE TO MORAL EXCELLENCE.

ON the crowded stage of the world — that area filled with the fleeting show of a vain and transitory life — how difficult, rather how impossible it is, to act up to the convictions of duty, or even to think with the independence of a rational being!

Bound by the seven-fold cord of worldliness, tied by the unseen bonds of custom, swayed by the hope of obtaining the suffrage of the multitude, the soul becomes a pliable and elastic thing, tamely delivering itself up to the reigning mode of thought or custom.

While the world lieth in wickedness; while the fashion of it passeth away: while the prince of this world is not the prince of peace — so long will peace and piety be found in solitude.

How many, who call themselves the servants of Him who passed through this world only to endure its scoff and threat, are drawn from their steadfastness by becoming the votaries of a world which knows not their Lord?

Yet they will say, "the world is Christian now. No heathen cruelty, no open idolatry now mars it. We do but walk with the multitude who keep holy day." Yes, the world now cries with ten thousand tongues, "Lord, Lord," yet what pride, what vanity, what selfishness will they be guilty of who follow the example of the so-called Christian world?

Some may say, does not the path of the Christian lay through the world? Is he to adjure society and flee to the desert and emulate the life of the hermit and ascetic? By no means. The Christian is to act his part in and profess his Master before the world. But it is to lead, not to follow. It is to tread its ways as He trod them — only in doing good ; it is to mingle among the crowd alone to bless them, and apart from its purposes, its fashion, its desires, to live lonely in the love of Jesus — singular in the service of God.

While man is a social being, and as part of a community, has social duties devolving upon him, yet is he, in his personal accountability, a solitary unit. Placed here for a little time, to prepare for an unending duration, the whole current of his nature to stem and turn into another channel; with graces to improve, to which he comes a stranger ; with propensities to repress, to which he is ever prone, it is his wisdom, it is his happiness, to disengage himself, as much as possible, from the careless throng, and surround himself with a rampart of thought against the seductive encroachments of a fickle world.

There is a nobleness of mind, an independence of feeling about those who break away from its enchantments and who dare to walk in a path of their own, or rather of their Lord's choosing ; they live, or they may live, alone with God, conversant with His ways, enraptured with His works, skilled in His Providence.

The world knows not the deep, pure joy of those who, withdrawn from the bustle and affectation of life, mount, with the angels of old, the ladder of God's goodness and look quite through the deeds of men.

It is in loneliness and comparative seclusion that the sweetest foretastes of heaven, the harmony of Providence and the beauties of the natural world are most deeply felt — most dearly appreciated. Like the raven's visit to the brook Cherith, or the angel in the wilderness who comforted Elijah, many a message from God is sent to cheer the heart that is sequestered from the crowd.

GALILEE.

What holy thoughts flow o'er the soul — what memories cling to
    thee
And ripple in thy flowing wave, thou blessed Galilee?
The mountain shadows from thy breast that chase the sunset
    rays
Seem sacred as the veil which hid the bright shekina blaze,
And every feath'ry palm whose plumes before thy breezes nod,
And cypress grove and cedar bough tell of the Son of God.
Thy verdant banks in beauty still their lowly lilies wear —
The lilies a Redeemer plucked — than earthly pomp more rare;
And many a grassy hill around where evening dews are spread,
Once canopied by angels, forms a pillow for His head;
And mountain top and valley green shall stand forever dear,
Where rung his silver accent, where fell his pitying tear,
There Tabor's snowy brow reveals the brightness where he trod,
When as a diadem she wore the glory of her God;
And distant olives — peaceful groves — embalm the evening air,
As floats adown long centuries, the incense of His prayer.
Thou chosen lakelet of my Lord, would I might gaze on thee
In all thy holy beauty, thou more than favored sea!
Methinks thy waters echo still, and to their rocky bed
Resound to His omnipotence, beneath His kingly tread.
Thy conscious waters knew Him, and thy midnight's breeze
    adored,
When pressed thy peaceful bosom the sandal of the Lord.

And bright and holy is the light which o'er thy wave hath
    broke,
Where parable and prophecy the tongue of Jesus spoke!
Thy banks seem hallowed altar-stones: thy sky a temple dome,
Those gentle banks in beauty made my Saviour's lowly home;
And though the Moslem's iron hand hath all thy beauty riven,
Yet flashes in thy peaceful waves the radiance of heaven.
Thy fallen spires shall rise again, and, behold, from each temple-
    dome
Shall ring in glad hosannahs clear, "the Lord has come!"
Forever vocal is the spot, and sacred is the sod,
Where, heralded by angels, moved the footsteps of a God.